Christmas Goose

by Geraldine
and Milton Harder

Illustrations by Lavonne Dyck

Faith and Life Press
Newton, Kansas

Copyright © 1990 by Faith and Life Press, Newton, Kansas 67114-0347. This publication may not be reproduced, stored in a retrieval system, or transmitted in whole or in part, in any form by any means, electronic, mechanical, photocopying, recording, or otherwise without prior permission of Faith and Life Press.

Printed on recycled paper in the United States of America
97 96 95 94 93 92 91 8 7 6 5 4 3 2 1

Library of Congress Number 90-84535
International Standard Book Number 0-87303-146-6

Editorial direction for Faith and Life Press by Maynard Shelly, general editor; copyediting by Delia Graber; design by John Hiebert; printing by Mennonite Press.

Contents

*Rosie had a special pet
goose named First Gosling*

1

Rosie's gosling

R osie looked pretty with her tight golden braids at the edge of her blue cap. She wore a homemade dress of dark blue cloth dotted with dainty yellow flowers.

A striped gray apron covered the front of her dress to keep it clean when she helped with the work. The apron had two large pockets. All the girls on the big farm where Rosie lived dressed that way.

Nine-year-old Rosie and her family lived out west with nine other families. People called them Hutterites.

Rosie liked summer the best. With school out, she had plenty of time to play in the warm sun. She liked to go to her play house and pretend she was head cook. The dolls sat at the little table and ate the tasty meals she and her cousin Elizabeth made. Sometimes a gosling poked his head in the door and honked for a tidbit.

"You can have a treat," Rosie said.

She smiled at the baby goose and looked for bread crumbs in her apron pocket. He was her very own pet gosling. She had named him First Gosling because he had been the first goose born on the farm that spring.

For Rosie, it was just as much fun to work as to play in summer. She picked peas and other vegetables in the garden.

Aunt Katie would say, "If you do your work well this morning, you may have a treat."

What Rosie liked best of all about this summer was to watch First Gosling growing up. He was the biggest and fluffiest gosling of all. Rosie had seen him poke his head through the egg shell as he was hatching. He was then a tiny ball of yellow fluff.

For a little while, First Gosling stayed in

the nest that was a small hole in the ground near the pond. But a few hours later, he was already trying to swim.

Besides bread crumbs, Rosie's gosling enjoyed the green snake grass along the pond. It was juicy and sweet. Now that he was older, First Gosling ate the hair-like stalks.

One warm day, as the grass swayed in the wind and the clouds made pictures in the water, Rosie's gosling met a snapping turtle. Rosie didn't see the turtle at first. Gosling's mother was sleeping, when something scared her. She woke up with a start. The other goslings were swimming nearby, playing tag. Where was First Gosling?

Rosie, who was barefooted, spotted the turtle and waded out in the water to rescue her pet.

"Hurry, Gosling!" shouted Rosie. "Hurry!"

Rosie feared that First Gosling would get hurt. His mother hissed fiercely.

Gosling's mother swam with strong bold strokes. She reached him first. Snapping

Turtle was ready to pounce on her little one!

The turtle was already licking his chops. He knew what a tasty morsel was in store for him. But he also knew how painful it is when a goose strikes. The hard knobs on its wings really hurt.

The sad turtle crawled into the tall grass as fast as he could. First Gosling swam close to his mother all the way home.

"You're not ready to swim in the pond by yourself," Rosie told Gosling. "But it won't be long!"

Rosie felt relieved to see Gosling safe and sound. She fluffed his soft feathers. And he faintly honked his thanks. Waddling on shaky legs, he went to curl up beside his mother.

That night all the geese slept well with heads tucked under their wings—except Papa Gander. He stood guard, ready for any foe from land, water, or air.

Rosie also slept well because she knew First Gosling was safe beside his mother in their cozy nest near the pond.

2

On pleasant summer evenings

T he hot summer sun had just set be-
yond the rolling hills of the large
farm. Tractors and farm machines were
carefully parked in the farm yard.

Black and white cows were resting behind the dairy barn and milk house. The
chickens had gone to roost and the geese
drifted slowly on the smooth water of the
pond.

Men, women, and children gathered
outside, sitting on the steps and sidewalk
of the longhouse. They enjoyed the cool

evening air. The day's work was done. They just liked being together.

Ten families live on this large farm or colony, as it is called. Most of them are related. Rosie liked living not only with her mother and father and sisters and brothers but also with grandparents, aunts, uncles, and cousins. Each family had its own apartment in the longhouse but all of them ate together in another building.

The families had just come from the schoolhouse behind the longhouse where each evening they gathered for worship. There they sang German hymns and a few songs in English. The minister asked God to bless their families and their work.

The sidewalk still felt warm. The younger children who had been barefoot all day washed their feet in a basin. Then they were ready for bed.

"Wash your feet once more," Rosie's mother told Peter, one of Rosie's brothers. "You must have been playing in the mud all day!"

Rosie popped dried Bing cherries and fresh sugar peas into her mouth. They tasted so good. First Gosling waddled over to see Rosie. As she petted him, he looked for crumbs in her pocket.

Just as the moon came up, Rosie saw a deer and her fawn walking in the field at the edge of the farm buildings. She heard a coyote answer another coyote with its own special howl.

Sometimes on a warm evening, Grandpa Walter told about his trip to Mexico. "Yes, we looked for land there," he said, "but here the land is better.

"Our land here is just like it was on our farms in Europe. So, we decided to stay here."

"I'm glad," said Rosie. "I like it here."

She leaned back against the house and felt happy as Grandfather finished his story. She ran her fingers along her braids. Her hair needed braiding only once each week—on Saturday afternoons after her bath.

Grownups began to sing a German hymn that the children all enjoyed, "*Gott ist die Liebe*"—God is Love.

"Yes, God loves everybody," thought

Rosie as she looked around at her parents, the grandmothers and grandfathers, her aunts, uncles, and cousins.

"And that includes you," Rosie said as she stroked her pet goose gently on his neck and back. Gosling rubbed his head against Rosie's cheek and honked happily.

Rosie remembered when Gosling honked loudly for the first time. He often honked when he was excited or angry about something.

Aunt Katie also enjoyed watching First Gosling waddle around and stretch his wide white wings. "He likes the crumbs and the singing," she said. Rosie wished First Gosling would keep on honking forever and that her big family could keep on singing songs about God and God's love.

Before she went off to bed, Rosie said a quiet thank you prayer to God for First Gosling and for her wonderful family.

Time for bed

The barefoot children wash their feet,
When it is time for bed.
They pop new peas into their mouths,
Before their prayers are said.

The crescent moon is hanging low
To catch the grown-ups' song.
A coyote howls, two fawns grace by,
The children hum along.

Their feet are clean, the stars smile on
The gentle folk below.
And all of heaven hears their praise,
"The Bible tells me so."

3.

The quarrels

"Joseph! Rosie!" Mother called. "Please bring a pail of potatoes from the shed. We need them for supper."

Pedro, the black Labrador dog, tagged after the children. He stayed close to Joseph because Joseph usually fed him.

"Don't you wish you had a dog instead of a stupid old goose?" Joseph asked, stooping down to let Pedro lick his face. "Geese can't lick anyone."

"I like Pedro," said Rosie. "But First Gosling is my favorite. You would like geese too if you took care of them."

Joseph teased her. "You're the only person I know who has a goose for a pet," he said.

Rosie shot back. "I don't care if I'm the first Hutterite ever to have a pet goose! Everyone should know my goose is special. Gosling knows me and likes me."

"Well, I think you're as stupid as your goose to have him for a pet!"

"I am not stupid and neither is First Gosling!" said Rosie. "Look in the *World Book*. You'll see. *My* goose is smart."

After they brought the potatoes to their mother, they headed for the colony library. Mother heard the shouting and wondered what was the matter.

"See!" said Rosie, holding the G *World Book*. "Here it says, 'These tame geese rank among the most intelligent of the many kinds of domesticated birds. For this reason, children who live on farms sometimes enjoy keeping geese as pets.' "

"Oh, so you aren't the first girl with a pet goose," said Joseph. "I'm sorry, Rosie."

"Geese are smart," said Rosie. "Even you could learn to love them."

"You really are a goose girl, Rosie," said Joseph.

Rosie smiled and squeezed Joseph's

hand. "Let's go home and see if Mama has some mint tea."

At home in the longhouse, five-year-old Peter had a glass of apple juice in one hand and a piece of dried apricot leather in the other. "How do you know what to have first?" Joseph asked, running his hand through Peter's hair.

Peter had been making designs with sunflower seeds. He just smiled the best he could with his mouth full of fruit leather. Joseph and Rosie sipped the hot green tea slowly. They smiled at Peter's antics.

"Peter, where's the button from your coat?" asked Rosie.

He tried to cover the missing button's place with his can of sunflower seeds. "Dan said his mom can sew better than mine. So, we pull and pull to see whose button stays on the longest."

"What will Mama say? You know she won't like to do extra sewing."

"Sew a new button for me, Rosie," Peter begged. "Please. I don't want Mama to see what I did."

"I'll do it," said Rosie. "But no more

button-pulling fights."

"Thank you," said Peter, giving his sister a hug.

Rosie wondered if she had gotten out of bed on the wrong side that day. She didn't like quarrels, hers or anyone else's.

"I know what I forgot!" she said. "I forgot to pray when I got out of bed. Usually, I thank God for taking care of us and I ask for help to be kind."

The golden haired girl with her cap tied under her chin was quiet for a moment. "Prayers really help keep quarrels away," she said. "Didn't Uncle John say so at evening worship yesterday?"

"I want to pray more often," Joseph said. Peter decided to ask God to help him not to get into quarrels.

The next morning, Rosie stayed in bed as long as she could. Her bed felt warm and cozy. This time she remembered to pray when she got up.

Rosie enjoyed her breakfast of toasted rolls and cherry jam, fresh milk, soft boiled eggs, and a dish of stewed apples and raisins. The children helped to wash and dry the dishes. Then, they set the table for lunch.

Afterward, Rosie ran all the way to the goose house with her pockets full of crumbs.

"I'm glad Joseph knows how nice a pet you are," she told First Gosling. "Aren't you?"

First Gosling gave Rosie a peck and gobbled up her pocketful of crumbs.

4

Why my goose?

S ummer and autumn days slipped by on the Hutterite farm. The last red and gold leaves had fallen. And now it was December.

Rosie knew that First Gosling could hardly wait for school to be out. He jerked his head this way and that, looking for her to come. He knew there would be crumbs in her pockets for him.

Humming Christmas carols, Rosie pulled her shawl around herself. She ran toward the large kitchen, across the road from the longhouse. She smelled the fresh bread when she got to the steps. Was it her mother's turn to bake? If so, Mother would give

Mother would give her bread with butter melting on it

her a piece with butter melting on it and some crumbs for Gosling. It was Wednesday, the day the women always baked bread.

Sure enough! Rosie found her mother taking the last of the crusty brown loaves out of the oven. "Did you have a good day at school, Rosie?"

"Yes, Mama. We sang Christmas songs. Now I want to take some crumbs to Gosling," she said, as she made herself a bread and butter sandwich.

"It's nice to have a pet," said her mother, pulling Rosie close.

Mama knew there wasn't anything Rosie would rather do than help take care of the geese. Sometimes Uncle John called her a goose girl, too. Rosie did not mind because she felt like a goose girl herself.

Mama filled Rosie's pockets with crumbs. "Stop in here on your way back," she said. "I want to talk to you about something important."

Rosie wondered what was on her mind. Mama looked worried.

"I'm coming, Gosling!" Rosie singsonged as she followed the path to the goose house near the edge of the pond. The pond was frozen over. In the summer, Gosling and his brothers and sisters enjoyed their daily swims.

"Oh, Gosling!" Rosie said, as she tickled him under his chin. "Was it hard for you to wait for me? I could hardly wait to see you. But I could sing Christmas carols all year round." Humming part of "Silent Night," Rosie threw crumbs on the ground for Gosling and the other geese to eat.

First Gosling was the fattest and biggest goose of all. He had the cleanest and whitest feathers. Rosie thought he had the nicest manners. But, of course, she always thought he was the best. Hadn't he been first to peek out of an egg in the spring?

As Rosie watched the geese pecking away at the crumbs, she wondered what Mama had in mind. Perhaps she had better check on it. Mama said it was important.

The golden haired Hutterite girl ran all the way back to the kitchen. Here, in the large central kitchen, the women took turns doing the work. The kitchen and dining rooms were in a building across from the longhouse where the families lived in their apartments. Men, women, and children had separate tables.

"Sit down a minute," Mother said in a serious tone of voice. "Uncle Paul told me today he wants to give the nicest goose we have to friends back East. Uncle Paul stayed at Uncle Leonard's home for several days during a visit. He wants to say thank you by giving the family a special gift at Christmas."

"But Uncle Paul can't send them my goose, Mama!" Rosie cried. "First Gosling is my pet!" Rosie's voice was trembling.

"Your gosling is no longer little, Rosie. He is a goose now. You know what happens to geese. Many of our geese will be sold for Christmas. Uncle Paul thinks your goose is the most handsome and wonderful goose on the farm!"

"Mama, please don't make me give up Gosling!" wailed Rosie.

"Well, the big truck won't be loaded with produce until next week. You will have time to think about it until then."

"I can't give up Gosling, Mama! Tell Uncle Paul to choose another goose."

"We will see, Rosie. Here, let me dry your tears. I know just how you feel. I had pets when I was a girl."

Mother gave Rosie another slice of fresh bread. But Rosie felt too sad and upset to eat. She did not want First Gosling to go away in the big semi. She wanted to keep him forever.

5.

Rosie goes along to town

After breakfast the next morning, Uncle John said, "I have business in town. Aunt Martha needs material for towels and sheets. And, of course, we will peddle eggs."

He looked toward the table where the girls were sitting.

"Mary, you can help with the eggs," he said. "And, Rosie, how would you like to go along this time?"

Rosie was excited. Her blue eyes sparkled as she said shyly, "I would like to go, Uncle John."

Uncle John loaded the pickup for the trip to town

The pickup was loaded with cartons of eggs, goose down pillows, fruit leather made of dried Bing cherries, honey, apples, potatoes, big carrots, and onions.

Mary, who was sixteen, helped Aunt Martha and Rosie into the truck. Their long skirts made it hard to climb up on the high seat.

It was a clear cold day in December. On the drive to town, the early morning sun threw shadows here and there on the light snow that had fallen during the night. The air was clean and crisp. Rosie noticed thousands of tiny rainbow-colored snowdrops on the stubble in the fields. She smiled happily until she remembered her sad thoughts about Gosling.

"Uncle John, would there be time to stop at the library?" Mary asked.

"Yes, I think so," he said in his deep voice. "You girls are great readers, aren't you?"

"I want to get a book, too," Aunt Martha said. "We can go to the library when we have our shopping and peddling done."

Aunt Martha smiled at Rosie. She knew

that good books were like friends to the girls. Mary, especially, did not feel right unless she had a book ready to read in her free time. She hoped to find a book by Laura Ingalls Wilder. Rosie wanted to choose a book about geese. Her teacher had said she could find one at the library.

When the pickup got to town, Rosie was surprised by the crowds. People flitted back and forth, shopping and getting their business done. After Uncle John helped Aunt Martha and the girls peddle eggs, they took the vegetables to market and bought material. Then, Uncle John dropped them off at the library and went on to do his business.

Uncle John found them there when it was time to go home. "Come," he said, "it is time to be on our way."

Rosie wanted to stay, but she also wanted to tell Gosling about her new book. She had found a book about geese. She learned that they can walk on land better than ducks or swans because their legs are longer and nearer the middle of their bodies. She also found out that their feathers are waterproof.

"They don't need raincoats," Rosie told Uncle John and the others as they got into the truck. "Geese have a gland near their tails that has oil in it. They press this oil on their bills and rub it over their feathers."

"Now I know why we call you our goose girl," said Uncle John, laughing. "You know so much about geese already. Good for you, Rosie."

Rosie's heart skipped a beat. It made her feel good when grown-ups noticed something she had done. Rosie looked out the window. It really was a special kind of day, so shiny and bright!

Just then Rosie remembered what might happen to First Gosling, and her smile quickly disappeared.

Aunt Martha noticed. "What makes you sad, Rosie?" she asked.

"Mother says that Uncle Paul wants to send my goose to Uncle Leonard," she said. "I want him to pick a different goose. Why does he have to choose my goose?"

Aunt Martha did not say anything for a few minutes. "I am sure it must be hard to think of giving up your pet goose, Rosie. Perhaps it would help if you would think how happy you would make Uncle Leonard's family on Christmas Day."

"Aunt Martha is right," said Uncle John. "You will feel better about your goose soon, Rosie."

Rosie tried to smile at Uncle John. But the smile wouldn't come. Instead she leaned her head on Aunt Martha's shoulder and reached out for Mary's hand. It helped to be close to friends when she felt sad.

On the outskirts of town, Uncle John stopped to pick up dozens of empty egg cartons to fill again. Then, he delivered the goose down pillows that someone had ordered. He also bought a jar of goat's milk for Baby Joanna.

Cow's milk gave Baby Joanna a rash. The doctor had asked that she drink goat's milk instead. Happily, Joanna liked goat's milk. Mary set the jar carefully between her feet so it would not break.

For awhile it was quiet in the pickup. Uncle John, with his thick beard, wondered if the colony should buy a new combine this year or wait until next year. They would need to pray about it.

Aunt Martha hoped she had bought enough material so the women could make all the towels and sheets they needed.

Rosie kept on thinking about giving up First Gosling. It made her feel too sad. So, she tried to talk about something else.

"Mary, did you ever wish you could have a pink dress?" she asked. "I wish I could. Some of the girls in town who are my age wear bright pretty colors. At the library, one girl kept staring at me. Why do we wear long skirts and aprons and caps and most other people don't?"

Mary put her arm around Rosie. "You do have a lot of questions, don't you? Let's see if I can answer some of them.

"I used to wish I could have a pink dress, and sometimes I still do. But when I wish for it, I remember Mama's words. She said that if we wear dark simple clothes and clothes that are alike, we won't be jealous or proud."

Mary smoothed back Rosie's golden hair that showed from inside her cap. "When we don't think about ourselves so much," she said, "we can do better work for our colony."

"I feel good when I work in the garden and make butter balls in the kitchen," Rosie said. "What I do is not just for me but for everyone."

"For we are laborers together with God," said Uncle John in his deep rich voice. He was reciting a verse from the Bible.

Rosie looked down at her pretty green apron with the pink hearts on it. She did not need a pink dress. Her apron was nice. Besides it kept her dress clean when she worked in the garden and played in the goose house.

"I want to be just like you when I am bigger, Mary," Rosie said as she put her hand in Mary's.

Aunt Martha's eyes looked thoughtful as she smiled at the girls. Sometimes trips to town were a good time to talk about important things like a pet goose and the Hutterite way.

6

Rosie helps Aunt Katie

Before breakfast the next morning, Rosie heard the women talking in the kitchen about Aunt Katie. "I am not sure what is wrong with her," Grandmother was saying. "She aches all over and has fever."

Rosie asked if she could take breakfast over to Aunt Katie. "That would be kind of you," Grandmother said. "Some hot cereal would be good for her."

Carefully, Rosie carried the breakfast tray across the driveway to the longhouse where everybody lived. Aunt Katie's rooms were in the middle of the long-house. Rosie knocked on Aunt Katie's door and walked in with the tray.

"Why, good morning, Rosie! What a pleasant surprise!"

"Here is your breakfast, Aunt Katie," said Rosie cheerfully.

Rosie gave the tray to Aunt Katie who was propped up in bed reading a book. The pillows behind her looked soft and comfortable.

"Grandmother says the cereal will do you good, Aunt Katie. I am sorry you don't feel well."

"I guess it is time for me to stop working so hard, Rosie. I am almost fifty now. We are supposed to let up when we are fifty years old, you know." Aunt Katie sighed a little.

"Then you will have more time to read and knit," Rosie said. "You like to do that, don't you? You knit the softest and warm-est slippers. I need a new pair again."

"Most of you children do," Aunt Katie said. "Your feet never seem to stop growing." Aunt Katie chuckled as she talked.

"I haven't minded the work," Aunt Katie said. "But maybe it is just as well that I ease off a bit. I do like to read and knit. Have you finished your book about geese yet?"

"Almost," Rosie told her aunt. "I'm trying to memorize all the new facts I am learning about geese."

"I was going to make butter balls and take care of the ducks and geese today," said Aunt Katie. "Perhaps you could take my place."

"I would like that," Rosie said. "Taking care of geese is fun. But now I have sad feelings when I see my goose. I don't want to give him up. I hope Uncle Paul changes his mind."

"I am sure you have many happy feelings when you think about First Gosling, Rosie. You have taken good care of him. That is why he has grown up to be a special goose."

"I will always love my goose," Rosie said, "and I know I will never forget him no matter what happens to him. You can't forget someone you love."

Aunt Katie tucked wisps of Rosie's golden hair under her cap, and did not say anything for a few minutes. She knew that Rosie would need more time to sort out her thoughts.

"I was also supposed to help carton eggs this evening," Aunt Katie said.

"Well, I can help to put the eggs in boxes," Rosie said. "I like that kind of work too." Rosie had a big smile for her aunt. "It's fun to help each other."

Aunt Katie's eyes had a faraway look. "I wonder if helping isn't the nicest kind of feeling a person can have. Thank you for the oatmeal, Rosie. It tasted good. I will rest a little, and then I will start on a pair of slippers.

"See, you have helped me feel better already."

Rosie sang Christmas songs all the way back to the kitchen. She wanted to skip, but she didn't want the dishes to bounce off the tray.

Rosie thought about the work women do. At seventeen, she would start baking and cooking. By then she would have a beautifully carved cedar chest of her own. She could put a rolling pin, kitchen knives, scrub pail, paint brush, hoe, broom, and knitting needles in it. The tailor would also give her cloth for dresses.

The boys got their own work tools: a spade, pitchfork, hammer and saw, and material for shirts.

Rosie put Aunt Katie's tray in the kitchen and skipped toward the goose house to wish First Gosling a good morning. "I think women have more work to do than men," Rosie told her goose, "but that is all right. We get more things to put in our cedar chests.

"What will I use first? I think I would like to use the rolling pin to help make rolls. But you know, Gosling, don't you, that I like to take care of geese the best."

First Gosling honked and whistled in agreement as he ruffled his beautiful feathers.

"Oh Gosling!" Rosie said as she held her handsome goose close. "I don't want to give you up, ever!"

When Rosie let her goose go, she told

him that she promised to help Aunt Katie. "I better get started, don't you think? But first I must clean your house."

The goose girl borrowed a rake from her mother and began cleaning out the goose house. She worked fast and cleaned all the corners. She saved some of the feathers to take home. How nice, she thought, when she could have her very own rake.

First Gosling stuck his head in the door and cheered her on. Rosie wanted the goose house to be the cleanest place of all.

7

Rosie tells a story

Behind the longhouse stands the colony schoolhouse. It is a simple white building with one large room. Only children from the colony attend this school. There are small desks for the smaller children and several larger desks for the big children. There is a table for the teacher in front of the room.

On Sundays and on week nights, the same room is also used for the church services by all the people in the colony. The school desks are moved to the side and benches are moved in for the church services. The minister uses the teacher's desk.

The Hutterite colony has its own school so that the children can be taught the Bible and their Hutterite way of life. They also learn reading, writing, arithmetic, and other things.

It was a crisp breath-blowing morning in December on the Hutterite farm. Rosie and the other school children were telling stories in the warm schoolhouse. The shiny clean schoolroom had frost pictures on the windowpanes. The Christmas scenes the children had drawn gave the room a festive look.

"Rosie," Miss Willie asked, "what is your story about?" Miss Willie's home was about forty miles away, so she lived in a mobile home on the Hutterite farm during the week.

"My story is about geese," Rosie said. "I learned some interesting things about geese this summer and from the library book I got in town."

"Good for you, Rosie." Miss Willie had a smile for her fourth grader. "When you tell a story, we usually learn something."

"I am going to tell about First Gosling when he was a baby," Rosie said.

Papa Gander and Mama Goose made a soft warm nest for their new family of goslings. They made their nest of grasses and feathers. Gosling's mother plucked hundreds and hundreds of soft down feathers from her body for a lining for the nest.

Mama Goose laid five large white eggs in the nest. Then she stayed on the nest to keep the eggs warm so that they would hatch. Sometimes, in the middle of the day, when the sun kept the eggs warm enough, she left the nest. She was hungry for a mouthful of fresh snake grass or a taste of the new wheat in the fields.

After twenty-eight days, the eggs began to crack. First Gosling was the first to struggle out of his shell.

Almost as soon as they were hatched, the goslings could waddle around. First Gosling cheeped as he pushed his way in and out between Mama's legs. Then he flapped his little wings and tried to climb up on her back. The rest of the goslings followed.

Papa Goose watched carefully when First Gosling tumbled into the water. Maybe he remembered when he tried to swim for the first time. First Gosling coughed and sputtered and shook himself.

Papa stayed nearby and told First Gosling what to do. "It's all right, First Gosling! I am right here. Why don't you see what swimming is like?"

First Gosling kicked his strong feet. He started moving through the water. In a few minutes he could swim and float. First Gosling liked the new feeling and cheeped happily.

The five big goose eggs were hatched when it was almost lunch time. In the afternoon, all the little goslings were swimming in the pond not far from Mama and Papa and the soft warm nest. Papa and Mama were

It was not hard for her to draw a goose

proud of their five little goslings.

"That's my story," said Rosie. "First Gosling is now a fine big goose."

The children in Rosie's class talked about Rosie's story. "I like your picture words," said Miriam.

"What do you feed goslings?" Paul asked.

"At first the goslings nibble grass along the stream," Rosie said. "Then I help to feed them stale bread soaked in milk. I also gave First Gosling crumbs. Later they eat grass like their parents."

"Your story helped us see just how Papa Gander and Mama Goose and all of their little goslings look and act," Miss Willie said. "You told your story well."

Rosie smiled happily under her dark blue cap. Before she went home, she stopped to draw a picture of First Gosling on the frosty schoolroom window. It was not hard for her to draw a goose.

Rosie ran all the way home. She knew that her mother would be waiting to hear how she did with her goose story.

8

The lost goose

"Row, row, row your boat, gently down the stream" sang the women and girls candling eggs in the warm barn.

"What else shall we sing?" asked Aunt Elizabeth.

"*Gott Ist die Liebe*," said Sarah. "That means 'God is love' in English."

"Yes it does," Aunt Elizabeth said. "It's nice to be able to sing both German and English songs. Let's sing 'Silent Night' next."

While everyone was singing and candling eggs, First Gosling ambled by.

"Do you want to come in and help with

the eggs?" asked Rosie. She reached out and stroked First Gosling under his chin.

"Remember when you used to carry him around in your arms? But not anymore!" said Aunt Elizabeth.

Rosie petted her goose while he looked for crumbs in her pocket. She tried to remember to keep her pocket full.

"Let's sing a song about geese," Rosie said. "Miss Willie taught us a Dutch song about ducks, but we could sing about geese instead."

Rosie sang the song.

All the geese are swimming in the
    water,
Fa da ra de rea,
Fa da ra de ria.
All the geese are swimming in the
    water,
Fa, fa,
Fa da ra da ra de ra de ra.

"That's fun to sing," said Mary. She held a large brown egg up to the light and put it in a carton. "Let's sing it until we learn it. I like the 'fa da ra' parts."

The wind whistled around the corners of the barn and sang along. Everyone's heart felt as warm as the warm barn from singing and working together.

After the eggs were candled, it was time for supper. Rosie liked the fresh apple crisp for dessert. After supper she helped wash dishes and set the tables for breakfast.

The mothers and older girls eat at their table, and the men and older boys eat quickly and quietly at theirs in the big dining room. The children have their own special table where they eat. One of the men prays before and after the meal. After breakfast and lunch, the men put on their wide brimmed hats and go to work outdoors with the big farm machinery.

When Rosie was through in the kitchen, she again stuffed her pockets with crumbs. First Gosling always liked a treat in the evening before he went to bed. Rosie sang the goose song all the way to the goose house.

All the geese are swimming in the water,
Fa da ra de rea,
Fa da ra de ria.

The goose house was warm and cozy and full of clucking sounds. Some of the geese were bedding down for the night.

"Here Gosling!" Rosie called. "It is time for your treat!"

But Gosling did not come, and Rosie did not see him anywhere.

Rosie's stomach felt as if tied in a knot. Her heart skipped a beat.

Where could he be?

He had watched her candle eggs before supper.

She hurried to the barn, but Gosling wasn't there.

She looked in the dairy barn, but she did not see Gosling in the stalls where the cows are milked with machines.

He wasn't in the cow barn with the cows who munched on hay and oats.

He was not in the potato shed. He was not in the machine shed.

Rosie could not find him in the green-house where Walter took care of plants.

She was out of breath when she reached the kitchen.

"Mama, where is my goose?" Rosie

cried. "He's lost! He can't stay out in the cold all night! He will freeze!"

"Calm down, Rosie," Mama said, putting her arm around her. "Imagine where you might go if you were a goose. You wouldn't go to the potato barn or to the cows. He likes two places best: your pockets and the pond. Why don't you check the pond?"

Joseph went along with Rosie. "I hope he is there," she said. "Maybe he was dreaming about a swim, but the pond is frozen. He can't even get a drink. And there is no grass to eat in winter."

Rosie tried to keep up with Joseph's long strides. Sometimes she wished she was tall and had long legs. It was dark, so they had to walk more slowly as they got farther and farther away from the yard light.

"Gosling, where are you?" Rosie called. "We're coming!"

"I think I see him!" Joseph shouted. "Mama was right. He must have been homesick for summer."

"It looks like he is in the water!" Rosie said. "I can't see his legs. Look! There *is* a hole in the ice! He must have tried to get a drink and can't get out!"

Quickly, Rosie and Joseph went down to the edge of the frozen pond. The hole in the thin ice where Gosling had broken through was only a few feet from the shore. Gosling looked cold sitting there in the water. He could not get out.

"Wait" shouted Joseph. "Here is a piece of board!"

Joseph laid the board on the ice with one end on the ground and slowly and carefully walked out on the board to where the goose was.

"Don't be afraid, we will get you out," Joseph said gently to Gosling. Rosie held her breath.

Joseph got hold of Gosling with both hands and lifted him out of the icy water.

"Good for you!" cheered Rosie.

Joseph carefully walked back to shore on the board with Gosling in his arms. Rosie wrapped her shawl around the cold goose.

"Were you lonesome all by yourself?" she asked. "Come with me and you can have some crumbs. It is warm in the goose house."

Gosling snuggled up to Rosie and honk whistled in delight. He could not have green grass or go for a swim in the winter, but he could have crumbs to eat.

Noisily, he checked for some crumbs in Rosie's pocket and ate them. Joseph carried him all the way home. He held on to him with all his might because he knew that Rosie did not ever want to let him go.

"I wish you could always keep Gosling," Joseph told Rosie. "I like him too. But let's sing because we found him. Don't you think that is a good idea?"

"All right." Rosie smiled through her tears. "We might as well enjoy First Gosling as long as we can."

Joseph did not sing much because his voice was changing. Sometimes it was low and deep, and high and squeaky other times. The biggest trouble was that he never knew how the sounds would come out.

Joseph began singing a gay little melody. This was a time to be happy because the lost goose was found.

Rosie hummed along. First Gosling seemed to enjoy the music on the cold walk back to the warm goose house on the edge of the Hutterite farm.

9

Saturdays on the Hutterite farm

On Saturdays, everyone on the Hutterite farm got ready for Sunday. The older girls gave the schoolhouse a good cleaning so that it would be ready for worship service. The women gave the floors in the big kitchen a special scrubbing. They baked dozens of crusty rolls and made wide noodles for soup. They prepared geese for roasting in the ovens.

Rosie did not like Saturday mornings. She always had a stomachache when it was time to kill the geese for Sunday dinner.

She ran into the house to bury her face in her pillow.

The women caught several of the geese that were pecking away at kernels of corn in the goose house. No one caught Rosie's goose because it was to be kept for Uncle Leonard for a Christmas present.

A little later, Rosie walked slowly back to the kitchen to watch Aunt Katie get the geese ready for the pans.

"Their down feathers make the softest pillows," said Rosie. "God made geese for lots of reasons. But I still don't want to give up my goose for anyone's table. First Gosling is a special goose. He's my pet."

"Your goose will make Uncle Leonard's family happy, Rosie," Aunt Katie said.

"One of the other geese would make Uncle Leonard almost as happy."

Rosie wiped tears away with the corner of her apron.

Aunt Katie finished wiping off the geese with a soft wet cloth, sprinkled them with salt, and put them in the baking pans. They were all ready for the ovens.

Rosie liked roast goose. But she wished

they did not need to be killed. She enjoyed hearing the friendly honking sounds in the goose house. Best of all, she liked to see First Gosling amble over to greet her. He knew just where to find her pockets that were always full of crumbs. Rosie did not want that to change.

On Saturday afternoons, everyone took a bath. The men had their beards trimmed. Rosie liked it when her mother brushed her long hair and braided it. Mama and she could talk.

"Now you are all ready for Sunday," Mama said as she smoothed Rosie's apron. "Have you learned your Bible verses for this week?"

"Yes, Mama. Mary and I studied them together. She helped me with the big words. We learned Psalm 24 this week."

Rosie started to say the verses for her mother. " 'The earth is the Lord's and the fulness thereof, the world and they that dwell therein.' " Later on there were words about having clean hands and a pure heart.

Rosie looked at her hands. They were

really clean now. She could not think of anything she had done wrong with her hands this week. Last Sunday, the teacher said it was important to help with our hands and not to hit and hurt. She had helped to wash dishes and to get eggs ready for market.

Samuel and Jacob put their heads down when the teacher talked about what kind of hands they should have. Sometimes they used their fists to fight. But they always became friends again. Their fights were short and quick. And they did not make much noise about it.

Rosie wondered if God minded too much about that. She thought it might be all right since the boys kept on being friends.

Everyone had clean clothes for the Saturday evening church service and for supper. On Saturday evenings after church, the people sang hymns and talked together. One of the older family members sometimes told the Hutterite story.

Uncle John said that their relatives came from Austria and Moravia in Europe. They settled in the United States and Canada where the farmland was good.

"Our society started in Europe about 450 years ago," Uncle John told the children. "Our people first lived together in Moravia, now called Czechoslovakia. Their leader was Jakob Hutter. That is why we are called Hutterites. These people had their own mill to make flour. They made their own clothes and sturdy shoes, beautiful bowls and silverware, clocks, and carriages. Some of our people were well-known doctors."

"When did the first Hutterites move to the United States?" Ben, one of the teenagers, asked.

"In 1874, over 100 years ago," Uncle John said. "It was too hard to live in Europe any longer. The government would not let our people worship and work the way we felt was right."

Uncle John said that their people felt that God wanted them to live and work and worship together. "Each Hutterite should help our big family obey God, earn a living, and be happy. That is why we say 'Our

Father' when we pray. Our life together as a colony is more important than what we want for ourselves."

Rosie looked around at everyone. There were aunts and uncles and lots of cousins and mothers and fathers. Rosie loved her big family, and she did not mind hearing the Hutterite story over and over.

Uncle Leonard had written the Hutterite story for people to read. Her goose would make Uncle Leonard happy. She wished that she could be willing to share First Gosling, but it was *so* hard to do!

It had been Uncle Paul's idea to give Uncle Leonard and his family in Indiana a goose for Christmas. When Rosie asked more about Uncle Leonard, Uncle Paul called him an archivist and historian.

"What is an archivist, Uncle Paul?" Rosie asked.

"An archivist collects books and papers that belong to church people and puts them in a library for others to read," Uncle Paul told Rosie. "You can talk to him about it the next time he comes to visit us."

10

When Sunday comes

On Sunday morning, the bell did not call the people to church. The preacher led the way and the people followed. Church was held in the children's schoolroom.

Rosie sat in one of the front seats where the younger children always sat. The babies and small children stayed at home. The older people sat on the back benches.

The women sat on the benches on the right side and the men on the left.

Everyone was quiet for awhile. Rosie

The preacher led the way and the people followed

was thinking about First Gosling. That is all she could ever think about it seemed.

After a few minutes, one of the preachers pulled his chair over to the desk and announced a German hymn. He had a songbook but the people in the congregation did not. After he gave the pitch, he sang a line of the hymn. Then the congregation repeated each line of the song after him.

Rosie loved to sing hymns. The singing was loud and clear. Rosie noticed that the women sang louder than the men.

After the singing, Uncle Paul got up and stood behind the desk. In a slow quiet voice, he asked the people to listen to the Word of God.

Sometimes Rosie's mind wandered during the sermon, but this Sunday she listened to every word. The verses were from the Bible, and Uncle Paul explained what they meant. He read a sermon from a book that was written in Europe several hundred years ago by Hutterite preachers.

Rosie heard Uncle Paul say, "At Christmas, we celebrate how God gave us his Son. He sent Jesus into the world as a little baby to show his love. Jesus was God's own precious child. Perhaps we have something special that we can share."

Rosie was thinking hard. "If God could give up his own precious child, I should be able to give up First Gosling," she said to herself.

Uncle Paul finished his sermon. His voice became quieter and quieter until the people could hardly hear what he was saying. Everyone knew that the sermon was over and it was time for prayer.

The people got down on their knees to pray. They looked up and folded their hands in front of their faces. Rosie kept on thinking about sharing her goose.

"If I give up First Gosling, I would be sharing my love with Uncle Leonard's family," she said to herself. She wondered if she would be brave enough to do that.

Uncle Paul's prayer was long, and he spoke quietly. He was not in a hurry to finish his prayer, and the people were not in a hurry to go. After the prayer, there was time for a hymn and the blessing.

The oldest man in the back of the

schoolroom left the worship room first. After all of the men and boys had filed out from the oldest to the youngest, the oldest woman left. Rosie was almost the last one to leave. The preacher left last. He was like a shepherd, caring for his flock.

After the delicious Sunday dinner of noodle soup, roast goose, and rolls, everyone took a rest. Later on, there would be Sunday school for the children and young people who were not yet baptized.

Before Rosie lay down for a nap, she looked for Mama and Papa. She wanted to tell them that she would try to be brave enough to give up First Gosling. She found Mama and Papa getting ready for their Sunday afternoon nap.

"It will be all right if Uncle Paul chooses my goose," Rosie said. "But it will be hard to give him up."

Mama smoothed Rosie's dress. "I know it will be, Rosie. But it is true that when we give up something we treasure, we feel good about it inside. What helped you decide to give up First Gosling?"

"Uncle Paul said that God gave us the

one he loved most of all," Rosie told her parents. "If God could give Jesus to us, I should be able to give First Gosling to Uncle Leonard."

"Good for you, Rosie," said Papa.

"Knowing you've made Uncle Leonard happy will give you a special kind of happiness," Mama said. "You will see."

Rosie was crying softly, but she was beginning to understand what Uncle Paul and Papa and Mama meant. Papa and Mama hugged Rosie and kissed her before she went back to her room to rest. She wanted to finish her library book about geese.

That evening Rosie walked out to the goose house and told Gosling how she felt. She stroked him gently as she talked. "I will miss you, Gosling," she said with tears in her eyes. "I will miss you very much." Then she buried her face in Gosling's feathers.

Gosling honked as if to say, "I know how you feel. I will miss you, too. But everything will be all right."

Outside the wind was singing its little song softly, over and over again. It was beautiful to hear. The big Hutterite farm was a place of peace and quiet.

Now Rosie was happy, too. She was willing to give her goose to Uncle Leonard. On her way back to the longhouse, she thanked God for the great gift that God gave to the people of the world.

Sing softly, Wind

Sing softly, Wind;
Sing softly to the geese
And their dear little goslings.
Wind, sing a little song softly,
And sing it again.

11

Rosie says goodbye

I n the middle of November, Uncle Paul had written a letter to Uncle Leonard that said, "I will be sending you a goose and some garden vegetables. We would like to share with you what we grow in our garden out West."

Now it was the second week in December and time to load the huge semitrailer truck with good things from the Hutterite farm. They would be taken to market in the East. On the way, the driver would stop in Indiana, to drop off First Gosling and the vegetables at Uncle Leonard's home.

Rosie would miss Gosling, but she had learned that everything has a purpose. People should work and worship. Good, quiet feelings come with work and worship.

Geese have a purpose for living, too, Rosie knew. God was pleased that she could have a pet, but goslings become geese. Their feathers make soft pillows, and their meat is tasty and good for people. That is part of God's plan for geese.

Mama saw Rosie hugging her goose. She knew how much Rosie loved First Gosling and how hard it would be to give him up. She was glad that Rosie was willing to share her goose with Uncle Leonard.

"Come here, Rosie," Mama called. "I want to give you a big hug. I understand just how you feel."

"I know you do, Mama, and it helps me to feel better," she said.

Mama hugged Rosie once more and smiled at her as she smoothed back her hair. "Both you and First Gosling have grown up so fast," she said.

The next morning, Rosie helped get First

Gosling ready for the long trip.

"You must be a good goose and mind your manners," Rosie told him, trying hard to keep back her tears. "I will think of you and miss you. But God gave us all a purpose, didn't he? I know you will make Christmas happy for Uncle Leonard and his family."

First Gosling may have understood. He fluffed out his feathers and held his head high. Rosie gave him one last hug while he checked her pockets for a few more crumbs. Then the handsome goose honked loudly as the big semi truck pulled away from the farm.

Mama pulled Rosie close as they watched First Gosling leave and gave her a handkerchief for her tears. "I am proud of you," she said.

Rosie smiled through her tears. She was glad for Mama's hug.

The semi nosed its way down the long drive and onto the highway.

First Gosling left Rosie and her tears and her home far behind.

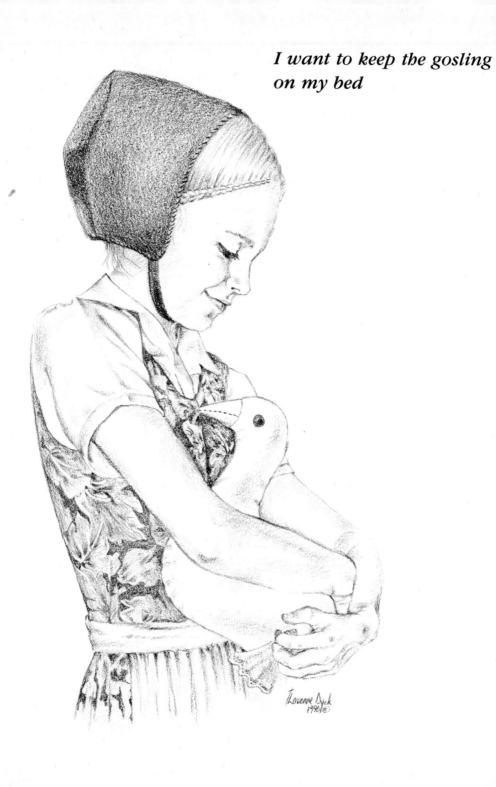

I want to keep the gosling
on my bed

12

A gift for Rosie

After a tasty Christmas dinner, Rosie wrapped a shawl around herself and ran out with crumbs for the geese. She knew that crumbs were the best gift she could give them.

As the geese ate she told them all about First Gosling. A few tears came when she mentioned his name.

"First Gosling had a special reason for living, Rosie told the geese. You do, too.

"First Gosling was my pet. And he was a Christmas goose besides. I think God is pleased with him, don't you?"

The geese honked. It seemed they agreed.

Rosie looked up and saw Aunt Katie coming. She was carrying something under her arm. Aunt Katie saw the tears and knew that Rosie missed First Gosling very much.

"Here, Rosie," Aunt Katie said. "I made a stuffed toy gosling for you. You can play with it until you have a new gosling in the spring. I want to give it to you for Christmas. I hope it will always help you to remember First Gosling."

Rosie stroked the toy gosling. It was soft and pretty. Aunt Katie had used all the right colors. The little gosling had blue eyes, an orange bill, and orange webbed feet. The fluff on the gosling was light yellow and there were a few white feathers.

"Thank you, Aunt Katie." Rosie gave her aunt a big hug and smiled through her tears. "When I am older I will put the gosling in my cedar chest, but now I want to keep it on my bed and play with it."

Rosie and her aunt watched the geese eating the last of the crumbs. There were no goslings now, but there would be some again in the spring. Rosie was glad about that.

Several days later, a letter came in the mail for Uncle Paul. It was from Uncle Leonard. He thanked Uncle Paul for the goose and all the other fine things he had sent. "Someone took good care of that goose while it was growing up," he wrote. "It must have been fed all the right things."

"And loved," added Uncle Paul, giving Rosie a smile.

Standing by the mailbox along the road, Uncle Paul held Rosie close. "You did a good job of feeding and loving First Gosling," he said. "Uncle Leonard's family will always remember your Christmas goose."

Rosie stuffed her hands in her pockets that used to be filled with crumbs for First Gosling and smiled at Uncle Paul. "I can hardly wait for spring to come," she said. "Then there will be more goslings to love and feed."

"That's right, Little Goose Girl! I wonder what you will call your next pet. First Gosling was a good name for the Christmas goose."

"I must wait and see the goslings first,"

she said, stroking her toy gosling from Aunt Katie. "But I will never forget First Gosling, Uncle Paul. He was a special goose."

"And a special Christmas goose," Uncle Paul said. Taking Rosie's hand, they walked back to the longhouse together through the soft deep snow.

Thank you

Thank you, dear friends on the Hutterite farm out West. You invited us into your homes and we felt the warmth of your love. We learned to know your children and you shared your delicious meals with us. We worshiped and worked together. We observed your geese on land and water, and watched all of you at work. Without these experiences, we could not have written this story.

The Hutterite families usually speak German among themselves. We have not tried to translate their way of speaking into English nor the way they address each other. But we hope that as you read this story in our everyday English, you will learn about another way of life.

We thank our brother Leonard Gross who has studied the Hutterite people and has written a history book about them. He read this story and gave us helpful suggestions. A Hutterite minister once gave Leonard and his family a goose for Christmas. His wife Irene told us about the gift. This gave us the idea for the story.

Thank you, Professor Lonny Kaneko and fellow creative writing students at Highline Community College, Seattle. You listened to each chapter we read in class and then gave helpful suggestions and encouragement.

We thank our friend Natalie Lessinger who joined us in the experience on the Hutterite farm and encouraged the writing of this story.

We thank Paul S. Gross (Uncle Paul in the story), who is a Hutterite minister and writer, for reading the story about Rosie and telling us that he was happy that it will be a book.

Finally, we thank our children Bob and Lorna, and Jim and Karen who enjoy pets and who also like to reach out to other people to learn and share.

Geraldine and Milton Harder, who wrote this book, live in North Newton, Kansas. Geraldine is a homemaker and writer. She especially enjoys writing for children. She has published a book, *When Apples Are Ripe*. Milton, who is a pastor, grew up on a farm. He has edited and written Christian education materials and articles. The Harders have traveled to many places and enjoy learning about the different ways people live.

Lavonne Dyck, who created the illustrations for this book, visited Hutterite people who live near her farm home in Viborg, South Dakota. She teaches art at Freeman Academy and often draws portraits of her neighbors and people she meets at art fairs.